THE ADVENTURES OF
THE
KETCHUP
KIDS

THE ADVENTURES OF THE KETCHUP KIDS

ANDREW BURTON

Illustrated by
Jacqui Bignell

Matador
9 Priory Business Park,
Wistow Road, Kibworth Beauchamp,
Leicestershire. LE8 0RX
Tel: (+44) 116 279 2299
Fax: (+44) 116 279 2277
Email: books@troubador.co.uk
Web: www.troubador.co.uk/matador

ISBN 978 1848767 942

British Library Cataloguing in Publication Data.
A catalogue record for this book is available from the British Library.

Typeset in 12pt Aldine401 BT Roman by Troubador Publishing Ltd, Leicester, UK

Matador is an imprint of Troubador Publishing Ltd

Printed and bound in the UK by TJ International, Padstow, Cornwall

To my two magnificent boys and the other real life Ketchup Kids who provided inspiration for this story:-

Luke "Champ" Burton
Michael "TGB" Burton
The awesome Tim Stackhouse
Tom "Whizzo" Jeffery
The delightful Sarah Jeffery

Thanks for all the fun we shared that lives on in the pages of this book.

Any likeness between the real life Ketchup Kids and the fictitious characters in this story is purely coincidental.

The Ketchup Kids

Chapter One
How it all Started

Luke skidded to a halt in the driveway sending a shower of gravel splattering against the garage door. He got off his bike, leaned it up against the wall and checked his watch.

"Hmm, not bad," he thought to himself. "Three minutes 22 seconds, a new Luke Kingsman 'round the block' record."

He rang the doorbell and waited. Two sparkling blue eyes appeared through the letterbox.

"20 pence and you can come in," said a voice. It was Michael, his younger brother and chief prankster of the Kingsman household.

"20 pence," spluttered Luke. "I live here. I'm not paying to come into my own house. Let me in!"

"Nope," said Michael. "It's 20 pence entrance fee,

1

or you have to stay outside for the rest of the day!"

Michael gave one of his infectious chuckles that made even Luke grin. "And… ," he said, "if you don't pay me by the time I count to ten the price is going up to 50 pence!"

"50 pence," shouted Luke. "That's a rip off. Let me in or else!"

"Or else what?" replied Michael.

"Or else I duff you up when I do get inside!" said Luke, getting impatient with his brother. Michael thought for a moment. He knew what getting duffed up meant, so he had a re-think.

"OK," he said. "Just 20 pence, no duff up and I'll let you in."

Just then there was the sound of more bike wheels on gravel and Luke turned round to see Whizzo, Tim and Sarah pulling into the driveway.

"Hi Luke," shouted Whizzo.

"Hi guys," said Luke. "Nice timing. Mum's just getting the food ready."

"Happy Birthday Luke," said Sarah.

"I've got you a wicked present," said Tim as he recklessly tossed his bike next to Luke's.

Suddenly the front door flung open and Michael, forgetting the negotiations he had been involved in with his brother, burst out of the house and ran to greet Luke's friends. He made a beeline for Tim and jumped onto his back.

"Have I got a present too?" he said. "It was my birthday three months ago."

"No, you cheeky monkey," said Tim, "I gave you a football for your birthday, you can't have another present!"

The five children bundled through the front door, where delicious smells filled the air. As they went into the kitchen, the children feasted their eyes on three large pizzas, covered with generous piles of pepperoni and piping hot bubbling cheese. A mountain of chunky chips sat enticingly next to the pizzas and within a few moments the children were tucking in.

Whizzo seized the ketchup and enthusiastically began to smother his chips with lavish dollops of his favourite topping.

"Save some for us," squealed Sarah as she saw the contents of the squeezy bottle rapidly emptying onto her brother's plate. In a moment of panic, she lunged for the bottle and started to tug it towards her.

"Let go, Sarah," demanded Whizzo, as he yanked the bottle back towards him. "I haven't finished yet, you can have it in a minute."

"There won't be any left in a minute," said Sarah grumpily, not letting go, knowing how much Whizzo loved ketchup.

And that was when it happened!

For the next few seconds everything seemed to happen in slow motion. As the warring twins tussled with the ketchup bottle, suddenly, a 15 foot jet of ketchup powered its way across the kitchen, heading for the door that lead to the hall. Luke, realising a crisis was unfolding, turned to see if his mum was watching but his eyes became locked onto his dad who had just appeared at the hall doorway. It couldn't have been a better shot if they'd tried! Ketchup splattered Mr Kingsman on the face with such a force that his glasses were blown clean off!

Everyone fell silent. Mrs Kingsman's mouth fell

wide open and the children sat motionless, stunned at the sight of Mr Kingsman standing in the doorway, his face dripping with ketchup and looking like he had been in a very nasty fight! The silence seemed to last forever as Whizzo and Sarah waited nervously for a reaction.

"Bulls - eye!" shrieked Michael, as he burst into a fit of uncontrollable laughter.

Before Whizzo and Sarah had time to apologise, Mr Kingsman marched across to the table, grabbed the bottle of ketchup and yelled, "Right kids, outside now, this is war!"

Whizzo, Tim and Sarah were not quite sure if Mr Kingsman was being serious. It wasn't every day that they were challenged by a grown up to a ketchup fight!

"We need some ketchup too," said Luke, standing up from his chair and ready for the challenge laid down by his dad.

Stuffing a handful of chips into his mouth, Luke made for the cupboard. Ripping the plastic off a bumper multi-pack of ketchup, he grabbed five brand new bottles of squeezy ketchup and threw them across the room to the waiting combatants.

"Pierce the tops and follow me. C'mon – quick, Dad's outside waiting," Luke ordered in a very grown up way, as if he were an Army Officer in charge of a platoon.

As Luke hurtled towards the door, he suddenly felt a tug on his collar.

"Oi, you," said his mum, "Take your shirt off now, and you lot too, I don't want you to ruin your clothes."

During the next few minutes, mayhem and chaos reigned in the garden as the five children took on Mr Kingsman in what was to become famously known as the Battle of Redwall (called that after the name of their house). Ketchup went everywhere as the children darted in and out of each other, all attempting to get a direct hit at their rival.

As the battle intensified, screeches filled the air and one by one, everyone became peppered with ketchup. Luke struck first with a six foot jet hitting his dad full on the chest and then he skilfully managed to dodge his dad's return shot.

"Wha-hey," he jeered at his dad and teasingly started to sing, "One nil to the Champions!"

It was then Luke's dad's turn to score a direct hit with a perfect looping squirt that landed right on top of Sarah's head, whose shriek must have been heard by neighbours for miles.

"Wha-hey," he shouted and then taunted in return, "You're not laughing now are you!"

It was Tim who discovered the splatter gun approach. By vigorously shaking the bottle from side to side in the direction of the enemy, he found that you could not only save ketchup, but you could also guarantee some ketchup would hit the target. It was at this point that Mr Kingsman started to look like he had a bad case of measles!

"Aaaagh," Whizzo yelled. "Shot by friendly fire!"

Tim, realising he might be to blame due to his newly invented splatter gun approach, spun round to see Whizzo laughing with ketchup filled nostrils and glistening red hair.

"Sorry," said Tim, as he dodged another attack from Luke's dad, who by now was shooting from a protected position behind the large oak tree that stood in the centre of the garden.

It wasn't long before the children started to close in on Mr Kingsman, who found himself cornered at the bottom of the garden, with five children pointing ketchup bottles right at his head!

"Do you give up Dad?" shouted Michael, with a wide grin.

"OK, OK, you win. Hold your fire and show some mercy."

"What's mercy?" asked Michael, who, being only six, didn't yet know what this word meant.

"Mercy is being kind to me and not shooting me after you have won."

"No way," chuckled Michael. "This is going to be the best bit!"

"How about we do a deal?" suggested Mr Kingsman, who was becoming desperate to avoid the final attack.

"You let me walk back up to the house without shooting me, and I'll let you all have double helpings of banoffee pie!"

"Tempting, Dad," said Luke, "but er... not quite tempting enough. Come on guys, let him have it!"

With further hollers of delight, the five children unleashed the remaining contents of their bottles and as they did so, a helpless Dad, no longer able to defend himself, disappeared in a sea of red sticky ketchup.

★ ★ ★

It took a good half an hour of hosing down before anyone was allowed back inside to finish their tea, which Mrs Kingsman had sensibly kept warm in the oven. As the bedraggled children marched back indoors, there was no doubt in Luke's mind that this had been the best fun he had ever had at a birthday party. And the day wasn't even over yet!

Little did Luke know that the events of that afternoon were going to change his life and the lives of his friends forever. The Battle of Redwall was just the beginning and, unbeknown to all of them, there were adventures round the corner, ones that were too exciting to imagine for a ten year old boy.

Chapter 2

Whizzo has a Brainwave

Now, there are two things that you need to know about Whizzo. The first thing is that he was very, very clever and the second thing is that he was also very nice. He wasn't one of those showy off kind of people who would annoy other children by boasting about being clever. He was friendly, kind and always considerate of other children.

Whizzo's real name was Tom, but because he was so clever, children at school used to give him nicknames. He didn't really mind having nicknames, but he did sometimes worry that some children wouldn't want to be friends with him because of his big brains. In fact, as it so happened, everybody liked him and he really needn't have worried at all.

He had been called Brains and Brainbox. He had also been called TurboHead, because his brain worked fast like a turbocharger on a car. He had even been called Einstein after the very clever scientist, which was the nickname he liked least.

The nickname he liked most, however, was Whizzo. Luke had given him this name because he knew that Tom's brain whizzed around super quickly. Luke thought that most people's brains worked at a safe speed of about 50 miles per hour, but he thought that Whizzo's brain worked at about four times the speed of most children, which meant that it worked dangerously fast at about 200 miles per hour. Luke sometimes accused Whizzo's brains of speeding, like a car breaking the speed limit, which always made Whizzo laugh. He especially liked this nickname because it was only his close friends who called him Whizzo, and because it wasn't obvious he was given this name because of his big brains.

On the night of Luke's birthday party, it was a tradition that his friends would stay for a sleepover. Like most good sleepovers, they watched a film together, ate far too many sweets, and chatted well beyond their normal bedtime as a special treat.

They talked and laughed about the adventures of the day, especially the ketchup fight; re-living the great shots and near misses, and remembering the great celebration they had when the battle ended in a glorious victory for the children.

"We really blasted Dad today, didn't we?" said Luke.

"He didn't stand a chance when we circled him at the bottom of the garden."

"True, but don't forget the traitor in our team who blasted his own team mates," said Whizzo, looking at Tim, whilst fiddling with the last remains of some dried out ketchup still stuck in his hair.

"I didn't mean to hit you," said Tim defensively, who then paused before saying, "but it was good fun seeing you with ketchup stuffed up your nose!"

One by one, the children drifted off into a contented sleep and by eleven o' clock, everyone was fast asleep. Everyone that is, except Whizzo, whose brain had not yet slowed down and was still travelling dangerously fast at close to 200 miles per hour.

Whizzo had enjoyed the day so much that he had already decided he was going to organise another ketchup fight at his house, if his mum would let him. As he was thinking about the next battle, he came up with a Whizzo super brainwave. Why not invent some special weapons for the fight? With excitement rising, as the thought developed in his mind, he rustled in his overnight bag in search of a torch, a pencil and some paper. Soon he was scribbling feverishly and wrote:-

Possible Ketchup weapons

1. Splodgamatic Guns - big guns for shooting loads of ketchup a long distance

2. Skid Pads - slippery blobs of ketchup to make people fall over

3. Ketchup Bombs - balloons filled with Ketchup which would burst when they land or hit someone

4. Ketchup Bow and Arrow - normal bow and arrow with special sticky ketchup arrow tips

5. Ketchup Rope - special strong rope made from Ketchup for tying people up or for climbing

6. Sticky pads - the opposite of a skid pad, a sticky ketchup pad that can stop people in their tracks

7. Ketchup Glue - similar to the sticky pad but used for sticking things together

8. Ketchup Spray Gun - a gun able to spray ketchup in lots of directions, like Tim did when he got ketchup up my nose by accident

Having written down all his ideas, Whizzo was still too excited to sleep, so he quietly went over to Luke and started to nudge him.

"Luke," he whispered, "wake up. I've got to show you something important."

Luke stirred and mumbled something but didn't wake up, so Whizzo prodded him again with his torch.

"Luke, wake up, I've had a great idea."

Luke opened his eyes and saw Whizzo grinning excitedly about three inches from his face!

"What time is it?" Luke asked, rubbing his eyes.

"It's sometime after midnight – listen – I've been doing some thinking about our ketchup fight today and I think I can make some special ketchup weapons."

"What kind of weapons?" asked Luke.

"What are you two talking about?" whispered Michael from across the room.

"About ketchup weapons," said Whizzo. "Look, I've made a list."

15

Michael scrambled over Tim and Sarah who were both still asleep, and joined Whizzo and Luke. Whizzo flicked on his torch and began reading from the list.

"Cool ideas," said Luke. "The only thing is, how are you going to make all these weapons?"

"I haven't got to that bit yet," said Whizzo. "I'm going to need to do some experimenting, but I've already got some ideas."

"Right, well, let's talk more about it in the morning when everyone's awake," said Luke.

"Okay," said Whizzo and with that, Luke and Michael quickly went back to sleep, leaving Whizzo to his thoughts. His brain was speeding up again. He was in inventing mode and it was exciting: splodgamatics, skid pads, ketchup bombs, there was so much to be done.

At last, even Whizzo's big brain had to rest and finally, he too fell asleep, dreaming of great battles that would be had with his friends. He was on to something, something big and exciting, and, most importantly, he knew it was going to be great fun.

Chapter 3

Watch Out! Here come the Ketchup Kids!

It was turning out to be another beautiful warm spring day and the children were sitting outside in the early morning sunshine, eating breakfast.

"Pass over your list of weapons, Whizzo," said Tim who was well impressed at Whizzo's ideas.

"This would be so cool," laughed Tim, as he read the list again and imagined shooting the Splodgamatic at Alfie Parker, the most annoying boy at school who was always bullying other children.

As he stuffed more toast into his mouth, Tim said, "We need a name, you know. Every gang has a name and it's about time we had one too."

"That's a good idea. Let's all think of some names and I'll write them down," said Sarah. "Then we will have a vote to see which one we think is best."

"I think we should be called the Redwall Warriors," said Luke, "because we all fought like warriors when we beat Dad and it happened at our house, Redwall."

"I think we should be called the Redwall Weirdoes," said Tim, "because that sounds scarier. Look, we could all pull faces like this and look weird and scary!" at which point everyone started laughing at Tim's contorted face which he had pulled sideways and upwards.

"Yeah," said Whizzo, "and that would be great for Sarah because she already looks weird and scary!"

"Oi, you!" Sarah shouted. "Stop being mean, Mr Double Weirdo. Anyway, I've got an idea. How about the Incredible Five because there are five of us and we can be a bit like the Incredibles!"

"Hmm," said Luke. "It's a possibility but I'm not sure."

After a few moments of silence, Michael said, "I've got it – let's be the Ketchup Gang because we are a gang and we are going to have ketchup weapons."

Suddenly, Tim and Luke, with eyes popping,

shouted at exactly the same time "What about the Ketchup Kids!" With this exclamation, everyone knew that there was no need for any further discussion. From that moment on they would be called "The Ketchup Kids!"

They gave each other high fives and Luke said, "Right, now we've got a name we need a meeting place."

"That's easy," said Michael, "the tree house at the bottom of the garden." Everyone nodded in approval. "And it will be a good place to store our weapons away from Mum and Dad," added Michael, feeling extremely pleased that his idea for a meeting place had been accepted.

"We need a leader of the gang too," said Whizzo sensibly. "You know, just in case we can't agree on something. There ought to be somebody who can take charge."

"Good point," said Tim. "I think that Luke should be the leader, because he's good at organising and he's fair if we start arguing."

"Thanks Tim," said Luke, pleased with Tim's vote of support. "Well, if you are all happy, I'd like to be the leader, and I promise I will always be fair."

And so, on that spring morning, the day after Luke's tenth birthday party, the Ketchup Kids were formed, with Luke as the leader and a meeting place agreed.

"What time are we going to the cinema?" said Sarah, suddenly remembering the plans they had for the day.

"The film starts at two o'clock," said Whizzo as he shovelled the last of his cornflakes into his mouth, whilst browsing through a copy of the local paper.

"Hey listen to this," said Whizzo. "You know Jake Heston from school. His dad's jewellery shop was burgled the other night. Wow, there was £50,000 worth of jewellery stolen from the shop! Look, here's a picture of Jake's dad with the police by the smashed window. I wonder if Jake saw anything. We'll have to ask him at school on Monday. Poor old Jake's dad, £50,000 is a lot of money."

"Guys, we've got three hours before we have to go to the cinema," said Luke, not giving much thought to the news about the burglary. "What shall we do?"

"Let's go into the woods for a while," said Tim who loved playing in the woods at the bottom of Luke's garden. "Then we can get back for lunch before the cinema."

"Sounds good to me," said Luke, and with that, the newly formed gang set off to the woods to play hide and seek.

★ ★ ★

Later on that evening, Whizzo planned to start inventing. His parents were going out for the night, and Jenny the babysitter always spent the evening watching TV. That would give him two full uninterrupted inventing hours in the kitchen, three if he could persuade Jenny to let him stay up an extra hour.

Whizzo's parents said goodbye and when Jenny was settled in front of the TV, he got straight to work.

He pulled out ten extra large bottles of ketchup and lined them up on the kitchen worktop. Getting these bottles home had been quite a feat in itself. He and Sarah had stopped at the shops on the way home, and after a big argument over how much ketchup was needed, had managed to sneak the bottles back without anyone noticing.

He started to read the ingredients label on the back to find out if there were any special rules for dealing with ketchup. Things like, "Do not mix with….," or

"Do not cook for more than 20 minutes," or "Do not get in eyes."

"Wicked," Whizzo muttered to himself. "No restrictions. What about the ingredients? Tomatoes, vinegar, sugar, salt and a few other bits and pieces. Good, nothing dangerous in there, time to get to work!"

For the next three hours, Whizzo worked away; mixing, boiling, frying, baking, chopping, banging, pressing, stretching and measuring; trying to get all different kinds of stretchy, sticky and slippy forms of ketchup. He noted down the ingredients for each

experiment so he wouldn't forget which worked best.

Half way through the evening, Sarah had come into the kitchen complaining about a nasty stench of vinegar. Whizzo had sent her immediately out of the kitchen, telling her if she didn't have anything positive to say she should go away.

At the end of his experiments, he cleared everything away, washed the pots and pans he'd been using and opened the back door to let in some fresh air.

He neatly stored the ketchup mixes in a variety of drinks bottles and tubs. Some went at the back of the fridge and some went upstairs to his bedroom to store at room temperature. He was confident that he had got the ketchup ammunition he needed. Tomorrow he would sort out the weapons.

The next day, he was up early and after a quick breakfast he disappeared down into the garden shed. He knew exactly what things he was looking for and it didn't take long to find them.

The Splodgamatic Gun was easy. He found his Super-Soaker Water Gun which was sitting on a shelf, a little dusty and home to one or two spiders. He took it off the shelf and started cleaning it up with a bowl of water.

"This is going to be perfect," he thought to himself. The box said the Super-Soaker could drench someone up to 15 metres away and could carry three litres of water.

Next, he started hunting for his dad's old weed killer bottle with the spray nozzle, which he eventually found stuck in the furthest corner of the shed. "Excellent," said Whizzo to himself as he examined the nozzle. "With a little tweaking this will become a deadly weapon."

With his ammunition and weapons now to hand, Whizzo ran inside and telephoned Luke.

"Luke, it's me. We're ready for weapons testing. When are you free?"

"Wicked, get over here as soon as you can," said Luke in a muffled whisper so no-one could hear. "I'll phone Tim and let him know we're on."

Whizzo and Sarah carefully loaded the ketchup weapons and ammunition into two large bags, strapped them to their bikes and then set off towards Luke's house. Whizzo could hardly contain his excitement as they pedalled furiously up the road, and he couldn't help ringing his bell madly whilst shouting to Sarah, "Watch out everyone. Here come the Ketchup Kids!"

Chapter 4

Weapons Galore

The five children gathered together again in the woods at the bottom of Luke's garden, each of them desperate to start testing Whizzo's new creations.

"Come on Whizzo. Get the weapons out and let's have a look," said Luke impatiently.

"Hold on, hold on," said Whizzo. "I'm just getting them out. Right, weapon number one – The Splodgamatic – a powerful monster of a gun, holding three litres of carefully diluted ketchup, with just the right balance of stickiness. This could stop ghastly Alfie Parker in his tracks with one powerful shot to the forehead!"

"Can I test it out," said Tim, who by now was bouncing up and down uncontrollably. He picked up the Splodgamatic and turned it on Sarah who shrieked and ran away at top speed.

"No, Tim, don't shoot Sarah," said Luke

protectively, enjoying the authority he now had as leader of the gang. "See how accurate it is by trying to aim for something. How about aiming for that hole in the bark of that tree over there?"

"OK," said Tim. He raised the Splodgamatic to his eye and said, "Ready, aim, FIRE!" and with that, he pulled the trigger and with amazing accuracy scored a direct hit, filling the hole in the tree with ketchup.

"Great shot," yelled Michael. "My turn, my turn," he shouted as he grabbed the gun from Tim. Michael had a shot and after hitting the target, punched his fist in the air in delight.

"Nice work, Whizzo," said Luke. "What have you got next?"

Whizzo passed round the Ketchup Skid Pads and Sticky Pads for every one to have a feel.

"The Sticky Pad," said Whizzo, "is ketchup mixed with a little bit of wallpaper paste and small pieces of super chewy chewing gum, baked in the oven at 220C for 17 minutes. Cook it any longer and it goes rock hard. Cook it any less and it's not sticky enough. Notice the bottom of the pad is extremely hard, like the bottom of a crusty pizza, but the top is very soft and squidgy like the top of a cheese pizza."

Sarah prodded her finger into the centre of the sticky pad. "Ugh – my finger's stuck! Someone help!

Luke held the bottom of the sticky pad and started backing away from Sarah. After three steps, the sticky pad finally pinged off her finger and rebounded back towards him.

"Woah!" he exclaimed, reeling from the force. "This is powerful stuff Whizzo. How do we stop them sticking to things when we carry them?" asked Luke.

"I wrap them up in oiled greaseproof paper," said Whizzo. "Now for the Skid Pads," he continued. "Made from ketchup, this is baked in the oven for 22 minutes to give a rock hard pad, then soaked all over with finest Italian olive oil, plus a little bit of regular ketchup to create the slippiest object in the world, the Ketchup Skid Pad; measuring approximately 25 centimetres long by 12 centimetres wide. Tread on this and you're history!"

"Wicked," said Michael chuckling. "I could use that in a school football match and chuck it under the goalie's feet to help us score more easily."

"Whizzo, you're a genius," said Luke. "What else have you got?"

Whizzo went on to demonstrate the Ketchup Bombs; small, medium and large balloons filled with diluted original ketchup and able to explode upon impact with its target. Next, he unveiled the Ketchup Bow and Arrow which was a normal bow and arrow with a small gobstopper sized ball of stodgy ketchup placed on to the sucker part of the arrow. Made with the same ingredients as the Ketchup Sticky Pad, upon impact, the arrow would stick firmly to its target and was almost impossible to remove.

Whizzo was especially proud of his Ketchup Rope, which had taken a long time to make. To get the right strength, the ketchup had to be boiled with wallpaper paste and glue, stretched and rolled into a rope shape ten metres long. When he had done three of these, he then had to weave them together to create the rope.

"This stuff is so strong I don't even think that the world's strongest man could break free from it," said Whizzo. To demonstrate, he tied Luke and Michael together, neither of whom, in spite of much wriggling and tugging, could break free.

Next, Whizzo showed the gang his tubes of Ketchup Glue. These were empty toothpaste tubes which he had re-filled with a potent mix of ketchup, a little bit of cement powder and superglue!

"This glue," said Whizzo seriously, "Can only be used in extreme circumstances because it is so super strong. It is impossible to get off clothes and difficult to get off hands and skin, so we must be very careful with it," he warned.

Whizzo's favourite and final weapon was the Ketchup Spray Gun, which was a ten litre container with a high pressure spray nozzle on the end. This weapon could eject either one powerful jet of ketchup, a shower of ketchup covering a large area, or anything in between. To get the power, there was a pressure pump which had to be pushed in and out several times before firing.

"Brilliant," said Michael full of admiration. "We are going to have *so* much fun. When can we have a fight?"

"First," said Luke, "we need to work out who gets which weapons and how many."

"Bagsy one of everything," said Tim.

"Me too," said Michael.

After some discussion it was agreed that each of the five children would get the following:-

2 Skid Pads each
2 Sticky pads each
1 Ketchup Bomb each

In addition, Sarah was to have the bow and arrow; Luke, Whizzo and Michael were each to have Splodgamatics, leaving Tim to have the Ketchup Spray Gun. The Ketchup Rope was to be given to Luke because he was the best at doing knots and lassoing things. It was also agreed that Whizzo should look after the Ketchup

Super Glue, because this was the most dangerous weapon and should only be used in extreme circumstances.

With the weapons shared out, Whizzo worked out it would take him about a week to buy all the necessary bits to make enough ketchup ammunition for their first battle.

"I'll need some money I'm afraid," said Whizzo. "Ketchup is blooming expensive stuff and we'll need lots of it."

"OK," said Luke, "I got £10 for my birthday. I can't think of anything more fun to spend it on so I'll give you that."

"I can give £10 too," said Sarah, equally generously.

"How about you Tim?" asked Luke.

"Not sure," said Tim. "I'll have to check my piggy bank when I get home – I should have £10."

"I haven't got £10," said Michael gloomily. "I'm sorry. I've got £3.42. You can have that."

"£3 will do from you Michael, that would be great," said Luke.

"I've already spent £10, but I can put in another £5," said Whizzo.

"No that's okay," said Luke. "You've already put in hours of work to make the weapons. We should be able to buy all we need with £33."

Sarah agreed with Luke that they would go to the shops the next day and load up with ketchup. It was also agreed that in a week's time, they would meet on Saturday afternoon at two o'clock in the woods to have a fully fledged battle.

The children knew the week would pass very slowly, except for Whizzo, who would be spending every evening cooking, constructing and refining his inventions. Even so, they all left happy, knowing that Saturday would eventually come, and with it, their very first official ketchup fight!

Chapter 5

Adventures in the Woods

During the week leading up to the first big ketchup fight, Sarah did some thinking about the forthcoming battle and was a little worried. She could just picture her mum's face looking at ketchup stained clothes. She was also very worried in case someone got ketchup in their eye which she was sure would sting terribly.

After some thinking, she had an idea and, with her dad's help, went onto the internet and did a Google search for kids army overalls. After a little searching, she found the perfect solution to her problem, a company that sold kids' army overalls for only £5. They also sold protective eye goggles and so she ordered five overalls and five sets of protective eye goggles for delivery to the house on Friday.

When Saturday came, the children met as planned at two o'clock at Luke's house. Armed with their allotted set of ketchup weapons, they marched down the garden and into the woods.

In previous adventures in the woods, they had built a base camp around the trunk of a big tree by leaning large broken branches against it, which made the camp look like a wigwam.

Once inside the camp the teams were decided; Luke, Michael and Sarah would take on Tim and Whizzo. Luke's team, the attackers, would start at the big dip. Their aim was for one of them to get back inside base camp without being shot. Tim and Whizzo, the defenders, had to shoot them down before they got to the camp. You had to be shot twice to be out of the game, because, as Michael had said, if you were shot once in a war you might just have an injury, but if you had been shot twice you were definitely "deaded for good!"

"Alright everyone," said Luke. "For the first game, we'll just use the Splodgamatics, the bow and arrow, the spray gun, and the ketchup rope. Leave the rest of the stuff under the bushes over there in case anyone comes by and tries to nick it. Are we ready for our first game?"

"Not quite," said Sarah. "Dad and I bought these the other day; army overalls to protect our clothes, and these goggles to protect our eyes."

"Coooool," said Tim. "Army overalls just like the real thing – we *are* the business! Let's muddy our faces like real soldiers," and he immediately started to wipe handfuls of wet mud across his face, making the others chuckle.

"You look better with most of your face covered in mud," teased Whizzo.

"Great idea to get the overalls, Sarah," said Luke. "Where did you get them?"

"Dad bought them for us. I said we needed them for some muddy games in the wood. We got them from a company on the web."

"Okay, Ketchup Kids," said Luke. "On with the glasses and overalls, and then give us two minutes to get to the big dip."

Once the children had clambered into their army overalls and put on their goggles, the two brothers and Sarah hurtled off down the path to the big dip. They slid down a steep embankment into the dip and hid behind a fallen tree trunk. In the distance they heard Whizzo's cry. "Two minutes are up. We're on our way. Prepare to die, you marauders!"

"What's a mal norda?" whispered Michael, who had never heard the word before.

"You mean marauder. It means someone who is raiding someone else's country," whispered back Luke. "We're the marauders attacking their camp."

"So does that make us goodies or baddies?" asked Michael.

"Goodies, I think," said Luke.

"Right, Sarah, you go to the left, Michael, you go to the right and I'll go up the centre. We've got the advantage of an extra man, so at least one of us should get through. Remember to keep low and wherever possible take cover behind trees and bushes."

The three children moved stealthily out of the big dip in different directions, whilst keeping a careful look out for Tim and Whizzo.

Meanwhile Tim and Whizzo had been plotting their victory.

"Right," said Tim, who assumed the role of captain of the team. "You stay here and keep guard. I'll go out into the battle ground and try and pick them off before they get here. They're bound to go past the hollow oak tree. I'll climb into the tree and then charge out when I see one of them go by." With the plan agreed, Tim ran off leaving Whizzo to guard base camp.

For a while, neither team saw the other. They could hear their hearts pumping with excitement. It was a strange and slightly scary feeling not knowing where the enemy was or when they would stumble upon them. Tim could hear himself breathing heavily and it seemed to echo loudly in the tree. He peered out from the side of his hideout to check if anyone was coming and just as he had predicted, he saw Sarah slowly creeping through the undergrowth towards him. She edged closer and closer... and closer... until...

"Aaaaagh!" screamed Tim as he threw himself from the oak tree towards the terrified Sarah, who froze in shock at Tim's blood-curdling scream. Within seconds he was only feet away, joyfully spraying her with his awesome Ketchup Spray Gun, soaking her from head to foot in ketchup and instantly taking her out of the game.

"There's no need to scream at me," said Sarah, still in shock from Tim's attack. "You frightened me," she said rather tearfully.

"Sorry," said Tim, a little concerned that he may have gone a bit over the top. "Anyway, can't stop. Off to blast Luke and Michael," and in a second he had disappeared back into the undergrowth.

Michael had done a great job of getting to within 50 metres of base camp, but, unfortunately, he didn't realise that although he was hidden in a bush, he'd left his bottom sticking out for all to see. What a perfect target! At exactly the same moment, Whizzo and Tim spotted it and repeatedly blasted his behind with ketchup, whilst screeching with laughter. With ketchup pummelling his behind, Michael reversed out of the bush.

"Stop, stop, stop!" he hollered. "There's no need to get me that much, you're wasting ketchup."

"Great work, Whizzo," said Tim, still laughing hysterically. "I've already got Sarah. That's two down, one to go. I can already smell a sweet victory! Just got to get Luke now. I'll go and hunt him down. You guard the camp."

Little did Whizzo and Tim know that Luke was on the verge of a majestic victory! Seeing Whizzo was not moving far from his position beside base camp, Luke had decided on an aerial attack and he had climbed a tree near to base camp. He firmly tied one end of his ketchup rope to a branch above his head and waited for the right moment to swing down and attack Whizzo from above.

When Whizzo was facing the other direction, he kicked off from the branch and, like a night owl swooping down on its prey, silently descended and landed behind Whizzo. Before Whizzo knew what was happening, he was suddenly being drenched in ketchup as Luke blasted his way to victory amongst cheers of delight from Sarah and Michael.

Hearing the noise and realising base camp was under attack, Tim quickly started running back to try and save Whizzo, but it was too late. Even from a distance he could see his friend was soaked in sticky red sauce, whilst Luke, Sarah and Michael stood cheering triumphantly in the base camp.

"Oi that's not fair!" shouted Tim as he ran back towards camp. "No one said we could climb trees. You …aaaagh!" squawked Tim as he tumbled to the ground.

"Yeowch," he cried. "That hurt!"

"Are you okay?" called Sarah.

"Yep, but my foot's stuck in a hole. Can you come and help?"

The children ran over to see Tim and sure enough he had got his foot stuck in a hole.

"It's quite deep," said Luke peering down into the hole. "I'll put my hand down and see what the problem is."

As he reached down, he felt tree roots tangled all around Tim's foot, so he began to untwist them and gradually Tim's foot became free. Tim slowly pulled it out.

"Thanks Luke," said Tim nursing his foot. "What a

stupid place to dig a hole. Why would anyone do that?" said Tim.

"Look and see if there is anything else down there," said Whizzo, who was still dripping with ketchup.

Luke lay down, with his chest flat to the ground, and reached deep into the hole, fumbling around to see if he could find anything.

"There is something down here," he said. "It's some sort of bag."

"Pull it out then," said Sarah, feeling a surge of excitement at Luke's discovery. "Let's have a look. If someone has hidden something down there it must be something important."

Luke slowly pulled out a cloth bag, his fingers trembling with excitement. The children were silent and gaping as Luke carefully opened it to see what was inside.

"Weird," he whispered. "Look at this stuff - a balaclava, gloves, a metal bar, I think it's a crowbar for breaking into doors, and a spanner." After a pause, he put the bag on the ground and spoke in a hushed voice.

"You know what this is. It's a burglar's bag that's

been hidden here."

The children stared at the contents of the bag, spellbound at seeing a burglar's kit for the very first time. It was Tim who broke the silence with an explosive shout that gave the others a shock.

"Yes! An adventure, a real life adventure for the Ketchup Kids. I've wanted our own adventure for ages and ages and now it's happening, I just know it. We're going to hunt down a robber and become superheroes and get millions of pounds in rewards. I bet we'll be on telly and people everywhere will want our autographs and everyone will think we're really, really cool!"

They all looked at Tim whose eyes were bulging and close to popping out of his head. Sarah got into a fit of giggles, never ever having seen Tim as excited as this and the others soon joined in, laughing at Tim's enormous protruding eyes and his infectious enthusiasm.

Luke finally called everyone to order and when the children had calmed down, he looked round behind him, checking that no one was around, before saying, "Guys, Tim could be right. If this is what we think it is, then we might just be at the start of our very own real adventure!"

Chapter 6
Wicked Plans

Luke picked up the bag again and looked at it.

"We've got to decide what to do with this discovery," he said at last. "I suppose we should call the police and let them know what we've found. What do you think everyone?"

Michael piped up first. "I think Whizzo should try on the balaclava so we can see if it fits him. If it does, then he must be the robber and we can take him to the police and he'll have to go to prison forever!" he said chuckling to himself.

"I'm not the robber!" said Whizzo indignantly.

"Are, are, are!" said Tim, trying to wind Whizzo up.

"Come on, sensible ideas only please," said Luke, bringing everyone to order.

"I've got a sensible idea," said Whizzo. "If we go to the police, then they'll take charge of the investigations and our adventure will be over before it's really got started, so I vote that we don't go to the police and instead *we* try and find the burglars ourselves."

"Here, here," said Tim, eager to support any plan that involved prolonging the adventure.

"I think we should go to the police," said Sarah, knowing this would be an unpopular suggestion.

Before she could be met with a chorus of boos, Luke stepped in and asked why.

"Because this might be very important evidence which could help the police catch some robbers."

"That is a good point Sarah," said Luke. "But what if we could find out more about the burglars ourselves and then go to the police with even more information? That would be good."

Sarah stayed quiet, still not convinced that getting involved with burglars was a good idea at all.

"Let's say that we don't go the police, we'll still

need a plan to catch the robber ourselves and that is *not* going to be easy," continued Luke.

"Let's catch him and blast him with ketchup," said Michael, pretending to blast an imaginary robber beside him with his Splodgomatic.

"Yes, I like the blasting him with ketchup bit," said Luke. "But *how* are we going to catch him?"

"Why don't we keep guard of the hole and see if he comes back to get his burglar's kit?" suggested Whizzo. "Then we could blast him, arrest him and take him to the police. Easy peasy!"

"Yeah and pick up our million pound reward," added Tim, who was still dreaming of glory.

"Not a bad idea," said Luke. "But we can't watch the hole all the time. We've got school and stuff, and it might be difficult to be here at the exact time the burglar comes. Anyway he'll probably come at night-time when we're in bed."

As Luke finished talking, they heard Mrs Kingsman calling them in for tea.

"Great, I'm starving," said Whizzo. "Let's get tea

and talk about this later." Everyone else suddenly felt very hungry too so they bolted up to the house, buzzing with excitement.

Mrs Kingsman treated them to a fine feast of crumpets and honey, toasted teacakes and fruitcake. The children ate heartily and soon finished. Fully re-fuelled and ready for more planning, they went back down the garden and climbed up into the tree house, which was by now, with an adventure underway, very definitely the headquarters of the Ketchup Kids.

"Now, where had we got to?" said Luke. "Ah yes, we were talking about staking out the hole and watching for the burglar. So what are we going to do if he comes back when we're not here, or he doesn't come back at all?"

"If he doesn't come within two weeks, then I think we should take the bag to the police," said Sarah sensibly, who secretly still thought that they ought to go to the police immediately, but also knew that no one would agree with her.

"Yes, that's a good idea," said Whizzo. "If we can't catch him within two weeks, then we ought to get help, after all we've never done this kind of thing before."

"Okay, that's agreed, if nothing happens for two weeks, we go to the police. You know, I still think watching for the burglar is not going to work, we've got to think of another way of catching him," said Luke.

For a little while nobody had any other ideas until suddenly Michael stood up and bounced around with excitement saying, "I've got it, I've got it. I've got it – why don't we leave some of Whizzo's sticky ketchup around the hole so when the burglar comes back, he treads on it and we can then follow a trail of ketchup back to where he lives!"

"Brilliant idea," said Tim, patting him encouragingly on the back. "You may be the youngest 'Ketchup Kid' but that's the best idea we've had."

"Whizzo, is it possible to make some ketchup with the right amount of stickiness, so that a bit of it would stick to a shoe whilst also leaving a trail of ketchup at the same time?" asked Luke.

"Hmm, it should be possible," said Whizzo, thinking quickly. "I think cooking the ketchup for about 12 minutes with the right balance of super chewy chewing gum should give us the right level of stickiness so that it sticks to the shoe. I'll work on it tonight and come back with more news tomorrow."

That night, Whizzo was busy inventing again. As you'd expect from Whizzo, he came up with a clever idea to try and get the burglar to leave a trail of ketchup. He baked a ketchup sticky pad, but made it a lot smaller, about three centimetres square with a thicker hard base than the one used on a normal size sticky pad. He then sliced a hole in the base of the pad and filled it with ordinary ketchup. Next he blocked up the hole with glue so the ketchup was sealed inside, and then he made a small hole using the prong of a fork, to enable a little bit of ketchup to escape every time the pad was squeezed. The plan was that the burglar would tread on the pad, the pad would stick to his shoe, and then every time he took a step, he would squeeze out a little bit of ketchup, leaving a trail for the Ketchup Kids to follow.

After a few hours experimenting, Whizzo felt he had got the perfect size and depth. He just hoped there would be enough ketchup in the sticky pad to lead the children all the way to the burglar's house.

By the end of the evening, Whizzo had made a dozen of the ketchup filled sticky pads, enough to lay them all around the hole so that hopefully the burglar would tread on at least one of them. In bed that night, with his brain whizzing round again at dangerously fast speeds, Whizzo found it hard to sleep, but eventually he dozed off, dreaming of catching burglars and being interviewed on TV about his brilliant inventions.

★ ★ ★

The next day the children showed up at Luke's house at eleven o'clock prompt, eager to see Whizzo's latest creation and carry on discussing their plans to become crime fighting heroes.

One by one, they hoisted themselves up into the tree house, clutching drinks, biscuits and sweets. After quite a bit of chatting about nothing in particular, Luke called the meeting to order.

"OK Whizzo, how did you get on?" said Luke.

Whizzo had a sparkle in his eye which everyone knew meant he had got on very well indeed. With every gaze fixed on him, Whizzo cleared his throat and grandly announced;

"Ladies and Gentlemen, members of the exclusive gang called the Ketchup Kids, I am proud to unveil to you this morning the very latest technology in fighting crime. This device, which has been years in the making, well, about two hours actually, will be a major force in combating crime for generations to come."

At this point, Tim, impatient and bored with Whizzo's big build up, prodded him with his half eaten Curly Wurly and said, "Come on, Whizzo, get on with it, we haven't got all day, you know."

"Alright, I'm getting there," said Whizzo. "Now, where was I, um, oh yes… for generations to come. I am proud to present to you the brand new Ketchup Blobomatic! A carefully designed sticky pad containing natural ketchup, which attaches itself to the base of the foot and then releases small blobs of

ketchup when compressed against the ground, thereby leaving a trail that can be followed by the expert crime busting gang known as the Ketchup Kids!"

Whizzo opened his bag and handed each of them a Blobomatic to admire and examine.

"Great stuff, Whizzo," said Luke. "Do you really think it will work?"

"Well," said Whizzo, "providing the burglar treads on one, I've calculated the range of the Blobomatic to be about one mile, so we should be able to track him up to this distance. I have made 12 so that we have a better chance of him treading on one. All we need to do is carefully lay them around the hole in the places we think he will be most likely to tread."

"Let's do it now," said Michael and within a second, he and the others were bundling down the ladder of the tree house and back into the woods.

After some careful thought and discussion, they agreed on the best places to lay the Blobomatics. They decided that twice a day during the week, once in the morning and once after school, Luke and Michael would check to see if the trap had worked and if it had, then an immediate meeting would be called and the trailing would begin.

With the plan set and the Blobomatics in place, all they needed to do now was wait and see if the burglar came back. If he did, there was no doubt in their mind the Ketchup Kids would not only track him down, but would catch him too, a thought that was almost too much to bear for five very excited children.

Chapter Seven
The Hunt is On

The next morning before breakfast, Luke and Michael raced down the garden and into the woods to check if their trap had worked. They searched round the hole and started counting the Blobomatics. When they eventually found all 12, both boys were disappointed.

"Never mind," said Luke. "It would have been very lucky if he had come the very first night. We'll try again later."

After school, once again, they hurtled down to the woods to see if the burglar had been. After a little burst of excitement when they could only find 11 Blobomatics to start with, their disappointment returned when they counted again and in fact had found all 12.

The routine of checking the Blobomatics twice a day was exciting to start with, but after nearly a week of finding all 12 on every visit, their enthusiasm began to fade. By the weekend, they had lost all their excitement, to such an extent that neither of them even wanted to bother making the trip into the woods. They had nearly lost all hope that their plan would work and so they began to take turns checking the Blobomatics, with Luke doing the morning check and Michael checking in the afternoon.

Meanwhile, every day at school, the others were eagerly waiting for exciting news. When none came, they too lost interest and they all began to think that the burglar would never come back at all. At the weekend, Whizzo and Luke checked the stickiness of the Blobomatics, which by now had been covered with bits of dust, twigs and leaves. Whizzo was worried that there may not be enough stickiness on the Blobomatics to attach themselves to a shoe, and so he spent Saturday afternoon cooking another dozen to re-lay on Sunday.

The following week, Luke and Michael decided to check the hole only once a day, together in the afternoon, because they had both become bored of doing the trip on their own. There was still nothing exciting to report to the others at school and all of them were now resigned to having their adventure end before it had really got started.

It was not until Thursday morning of the second week that something happened. During morning break time at school, Tim was playing football with some friends, including Jake Heston, the boy whose father's jewellery shop had been broken into a few weeks before. After break time, as they were going back into class, Tim asked Jake if he was feeling okay because he looked a little gloomy. Jake told Tim that last night, his father's shop had been broken into again and more jewels had been stolen. This time the thieves had taken about £20,000 of jewels! His mum and dad were really worried because they didn't know if they would be able to keep the shop going if the burglaries continued. Worse still, the police had no clues and they didn't know if they would ever be able to find the culprit.

On hearing this news, Tim's heart started pumping fast. Although he felt sorry for Jake and his parents, he was sure that the adventure was hotting up again, convinced that the person who had burgled Jake's shop was the very same person they were looking for. Maybe the burglar had come back to the hole to pick up his kit? He could hardly wait to tell the others. During the next lesson, which was silent reading, Tim secretly scribbled notes to the four members of the Ketchup Kids. His note read:-

TOP SECRET MESSAGE

*I have some important news about you know what!
Meet me at the plant pots by the school gate at
lunchtime. Don't say a word to anyone!*

From Tim

Tim then pretended he needed the toilet and when
Mrs O'Neill said he could go, he wove his way to the
classroom door, quietly slipping notes to Whizzo, Luke
and Sarah as he went past their desks, whilst giving
them a secret wink at the same time.

Mrs O'Neill looked up just in time to see Tim
wink at Sarah and she frowned at Tim for interrupting
the others. Tim quickly exited the classroom and
breathed a sigh of relief that she hadn't seen him drop
off the note.

When lunchtime came, Tim ran to Michael's
classroom to sneak him his note and caught him just as
he was leaving for lunch. At last, the gang gathered
together at the plant pots.

"Come on then - spill the beans," said Luke to
Tim, whose eyes were again bulging and looking as if
they were about to burst out of their sockets.

"There's been another burglary at Jake's dads' shop," he whispered urgently. "It happened last night. Jake said they broke in through a small window at the back of the shop and stole about another £20,000 worth of jewellery. Do you think it's our burglar at it again?"

On hearing this dramatic news, the other children were now as wide-eyed and as excited as Tim.

"It must be!" said Luke, thinking quickly. "I tell you what, after school let's ask our mums if you can come back for tea and then we'll ask if we can buy some sweets at Barton's Newsagents, which is only about three shops up from the jewellery shop. When we've bought our sweets, we can have a quick look round and see if we can find any clues. Then we'll go back to the woods and check the Blobomatics."

Everyone immediately liked Luke's plan, but they all knew persuading their mums to allow a last minute tea would be tricky.

After school, the three mums were quite taken aback at the children's desperate pleas to all go back to Luke and Michael's for tea. After five minutes persuading and pleading, the mums gave in and the children were allowed to go. Persuading Luke's mum to stop at Barton's sweet shop was even harder but somehow they managed to convince her that this was a good idea.

When Mrs Kingsman had parked the car, the children hopped out and quickly bought a bag of "Pick 'N Mix" sweets and then casually wandered three shops down to Heston's Jewellery Shop, trying not to look in the least bit suspicious.

The shop was open as usual and the only thing that was different was a notice in the window which Sarah spotted. It said "Reward" in big capital letters and she read the rest of the notice out loud to the others. It said:-

"Dear Customer,

You may know that we have had two burglaries recently. We are offering a reward of £1,000 to anyone who can provide information leading to the capture of the burglars. Please report any information to Police Officer Crammond at Hambleside Police Station on 01652 789489."

"Wow," said Tim. "£1,000 spondoolas – not bad at all!"

"How much is that each," said Michael, eager to know his share of the reward.

"£200 each," said Whizzo.

"£200?" squeaked Michael. "That's loads – we'll be rich!" he said laughing.

"Yes if we catch him but we still haven't got any real clues yet to help us find out who the burglar is," said Sarah. "Let's look round the back and see where they broke in."

As they were all marching round the side of the shop, Luke shouted, "Stop everyone – look!" He pointed to the floor at a trail of red blotches.

There was a series of gasps from the children. Luke bent down to take a closer look, and touched a blob with his finger. As he put his finger to his nose, there was the unmistakable smell of ketchup. He moved forward a couple of paces to the next blob, which also proved to be ketchup. He moved forward again to find a third blob of sticky red ketchup. With a serious look on his face, he lifted his head and said,

"Guys, it's ketchup alright. Whizzo – your Blobomatic has worked!"

Sarah jumped onto Whizzo's back, shrieking, "Whizzo, you're a genius." Michael meanwhile was

now doing one of his famous 'happy' dances which involved bobbing up and down to imaginary rap music and Tim had gone starry-eyed, dreaming of what he could do with his £200!

After the commotion had died down, they followed the trail to the back of the building where they spotted the broken and boarded window. It was about head height with a blue painted window frame. The children could just see where the burglar had forced the window open, probably using the very crowbar they had found in the woods.

They had a look around the area at the back of the shop to see if they could find any more traces of ketchup. After a minute searching, Michael discovered a vital clue. Whilst hunting in the bushes, he spotted a rather squashed looking Blobomatic which must have fallen off the burglar's shoe as he was climbing over the hedge trying to get away from the scene of the crime.

"Luke," he called, "come and look at this, I've found the Blobomatic." He carefully picked it up and passed it to Luke.

"Great work, Michael. We need to keep this for evidence," said Luke. "I'm surprised the police didn't find this!"

"Let me have a look," said Whizzo. "Hmm, brilliant, this is a better tracking device than I ever thought. Look everyone, the imprint of the burglar's shoe is embedded in the Blobomatic. This is a massive clue. If we can find the burglar, this imprint will be the proof that we have got the right man!"

Whizzo carefully put the Blobomatic into his pocket and the children rushed back to the car.

"What took you children so long? I almost came to

find you," said Luke's mum.

"We couldn't decide on what sweets we wanted and then we wanted to see if we could see Jake in his dad's shop," said Michael.

"I heard the shop was burgled again," said Mrs Kingsman. "The poor family, it must be so distressing for them, I just hope they catch the person who's done it."

Luke blushed and glowered at Michael for mentioning the shop.

No one said a word about their discovery; they were now desperate to get back to the woods to see what they would find there.

Chapter Eight
More Clues

Back at home, the children had a quick drink and some biscuits and then they ran full pelt down through the garden and into the woods.

As they approached the area where the hole was situated, they slowed down, just in case the burglar was still around. They also wanted to make sure that they didn't disturb any vital clues that they might find there. Luke started counting up the Blobomatics and to their surprise, the news was better than they had hoped for. They could only find ten Blobomatics and so, whilst they couldn't be sure, it looked like the burglar had trodden on two of them, one of which they had already found.

"Let's have a look in the hole and see if we can find the bag," said Whizzo.

Luke lay down on his chest and reached into the hole.

"There's probably nothing in here. He wouldn't have returned it this quickly and he may not return it at all this time," said Luke. "Hold on... it's here, I've got it."

Luke hauled the bag out of the hole and was just about to put his hand into it when Tim said, "Wait, don't touch the crowbar with your bare hands, Luke, the burglar might have left his fingerprints on it. Only touch it using a cloth, or use the balaclava if it's still in there."

Luke carefully opened the bag and inside he found exactly the same items as before; the balaclava, the metal crowbar, a spanner and some gloves. Luke emptied them onto the ground, without touching them.

The children were all silent as they realised they were in possession of some very important evidence to do with the robbery of Heston's Jewellery Shop.

Sarah was the first to speak. "I really think we ought to go to the police now. We've done a great job finding the burglar's kit and setting the Blobomatic trap. We should let the police deal with this now."

"No way," said Tim. "If they are prepared to pay £1,000 for information, imagine how much dosh we would get if we actually caught the burglars! Ha – we'll probably get about a million pounds each!"

"I don't think so, Tim," said Luke. "They've only stolen £70,000 of jewellery so we wouldn't get a million pounds. Anyway we're not doing this for the money; we're doing this because it's a brilliant adventure and because we want to help Jake and his family."

"Are we?" said Tim looking surprised. "I'm doing it for the money." He paused and then said, "Nah, you're right we're not doing it for the money, but the money would be cool!"

"I don't want to go to the police yet," said Whizzo. "This adventure is really exciting. We've done better than the police so far. Let's see if we can come up with another plan to find the burglar first."

Luke suddenly had a thought.

"Hey guys, listen. What if the burglar trod on one of the Blobomatics when he picked up the bag to go and do the robbery, and then he trod on the second one when he came back to hide it again. We know the first one ended up at the scene of the crime. Maybe the second one will lead us to his house?"

"You may be right, Luke," said Whizzo. "Let's spread out and see if we can find two trails."

"Wait a minute, I'll just put the burglar's stuff back into the bag," said Luke.

Just as he was about to put it back Sarah squealed, "Luke, look!" whilst pointing to the crowbar.

"What?" said Luke, not sure what he was supposed to be seeing.

"There, on the end of the crowbar – some blue paint – just like the colour on the window frame," said Sarah.

Luke gave a low whistle. "Well, if we weren't already sure enough that this was the burglar's bag, we certainly are now. We have even more evidence to give to the police!" said Luke, smiling as he carefully put everything back into the bag.

"I don't think we should leave this in the hole any more, in case the burglar takes it and doesn't bring it back. This is important evidence for when we go to the police, so we'll hide it in our tree house."

After Luke had put the bag in the tree house, the

children started scouring the ground to see if they could find a trail. It was much harder to see blobs of ketchup on the earth in the woods than it was on the pavement outside the shop.

After about 20 minutes, Tim found a trail that headed up one path that led out of the woods and towards the town. The town was about half a mile from where they were, so Whizzo was very pleased to realise that the Blobomatic worked for at least that distance, and maybe even longer.

"Whizzo and Tim, you go and follow that trail to the road to check it's the one that leads in to town. The three of us will keep hunting for the other trail." said Luke. "Meet back here in 20 minutes."

Whizzo and Tim headed off up the path in the woods, leaving the other three to try and find a second trail. Luke, Sarah and Michael searched and searched without much luck. Just as they were beginning to lose heart, they heard Tim running back towards them at top speed.

"Guys, guys," shouted Tim, "we've found the second trail, come here - quick."

Luke, Sarah and Michael ran up the path to meet Tim, who between gasps said, "We got to the end of the path where the woods join the road and then we found the trail we'd been following split into two. The burglar must have left the woods using the same path and then when he got to the end of the woods, one time he went left into town to do the robbery and then the second time he went right to go somewhere else, probably back to his house."

"Awesome news!" said Luke as the four of them raced through the woods to meet up with Whizzo, who was waiting by the road where the two trails of ketchup split and went their separate ways.

"I think we should all follow this trail," said Whizzo after they had all arrived. "We know this one goes into town but we don't know where this one leads. Have we got time to go now before tea?" he asked sensibly, not wanting to upset Mrs Kingsman by being late.

"We're okay," said Luke. "Tea is at half past five so we've got an hour, let's carry on. Anyway it's too exciting to turn back now."

So the children marched on, following the trail along the footpath. When it suddenly disappeared, they realised the burglar must have crossed the road. Sure enough, they picked up the trail again on the other side. The blobs of ketchup were very small, about the

size of an ant, occasionally a little larger, about the size of a small beetle. They had to keep a very close eye on where the trail went.

Eventually, after about half a mile, the tarmac footpath came to an end, as did the houses, and it turned into a little footpath along a grassy bank, by the side of what was now a country lane.

"This is worrying," said Whizzo. "We must be a half a mile from the hole where the trail started and the next village is about two miles away. The trail will come to an end soon and we'll lose him."

The ketchup trail soon broke away from the country road and lead up a little farm lane.

"Isn't this Sally and Freddie's farm?" said Sarah. "They go to our school and they're in Michael's class. Surely they can't be the burglars?" said Sarah.

"It probably isn't them but it could be someone who works on the farm," said Luke. "Let's keep going."

But at that point the trail came to an end, much to the disappointment of the children. Time was running out too, and so the children turned round and, half walking, half jogging, they went back down the road and towards Luke's house. Sarah couldn't help glancing back a few times just to check they weren't being followed, worried about an encounter with a burglar who they seemed to be closing in on.

The children felt exhausted from the excitement and were glad to tuck into large helpings of toad in the hole. They chatted and laughed over tea, gradually gathering energy again and looking forward to talking about the day's adventures.

"Can we have our ice cream in the tree house?" asked Luke.

"Yes you can, but you've only got 20 minutes before it's time for everyone to go home," said Mrs Kingsman.

The children wasted no time in going down the garden and into the tree house so they could talk about what to do next.

"What a day!" said Whizzo. "So much has happened – Tim heard from Jake about the second burglary, we investigated the scene of the crime and found the trail and a Blobomatic with a shoeprint on it. We found proof that the crowbar in the burglar's bag in the woods was the exact one used for the Heston Jewellery robbery *and* we found a second trail that led to Willow Tree Farm. I think we can safely say it's been a good day for the Ketchup Kids!"

Everyone agreed it certainly had been a very good day indeed. The next challenge was for the children to work out a way of actually finding and catching the burglar. This was such a big challenge that they decided they would meet again on Saturday afternoon to come up with a plan.

So, tired and happy, they went their own ways once again, with each of them plotting the next step in their great adventure.

Chapter Nine
Suspects!

After Saturday morning football, the five friends met for a picnic lunch at Luke and Michael's house to talk about their plans for catching the burglars.

"So what should we do next then?" asked Sarah. "Who's got a good idea?"

"I have an idea," said Tim. "Let's have another sandwich, that last one was well tasty!"

"No, I mean ideas about catching the burglar, silly. How are we going to find him and catch him?" asked Sarah.

"Well," said Luke, "first we need to find out if anyone lives on the farm other than Sally and Freddie's family. If we found that out, we could draw up a list of suspects."

"What's a suspect?" asked Michael.

"It's a well dodgy person who you think might be the burglar," said Tim. "Someone like Whizzo!" he chuckled.

"I'm not well dodgy," said Whizzo, defensively.

"Yes you are, you nicked one of my toffee bonbons once so that means you are well dodgy and we should include *you* on our list of suspects!" said Tim, pointing his finger accusingly.

"Well you took my Kit Kat at school the other day, so that must mean you are well dodgy too!" replied Whizzo.

"Fair point," said Tim. "Right, I'm a suspect too – what about Luke – he *looks* well dodgy so we ought to put him on our list of suspects!"

"I don't look well dodgy," said Luke who was laughing at Whizzo and Tim's banter. "But, the only person here who looks well dodgy *and* has a criminal record for stealing sweets is you, Tim. Arrest him everyone!"

Within a second everyone had bundled on Tim and were cheering and celebrating that they had caught the Heston Jewellery Shop burglar!

After they had calmed down and let Tim go, Michael, still laughing, said, "It's a shame that Tim isn't the burglar because if he was, we would only have to share out the reward between four of us, so we'd all get more money!

"Thanks a lot, Michael," said Tim. "So you'd like to see me locked up for an extra 50 pounds? Right, since you've all picked on me, that last sandwich is mine," and with that, he grabbed the sandwich and shoved it into his mouth in one go before anyone could complain.

"Come on you lot," said Sarah. "What are we going to do next?"

"I think we should talk to Freddie and Sally on Monday and find out about all the people who work on their farm and make a list of suspects, like Luke said," suggested Whizzo.

"Michael, you're in their class, do you think you could find out this information by yourself without letting them know why we want to know?" asked Luke.

"Of course I can," said Michael. "I am only six but I am quite clever. I can do it."

"Are you sure?" asked Luke. "We don't want them to suspect anything."

Michael nodded, realising that he had a very important job ahead, one that he needed to take very seriously.

"OK, Michael, you try and find out something on Monday morning and we'll meet at lunchtime to see if there is any news."

With the plan agreed, the children stopped thinking about burglars and adventures, and spent the rest of the afternoon racing around on their bikes, doing jumps and wheelies and narrowly avoiding crashing into each other.

Monday came around soon enough and unusually,

Michael was dressed early and ready to set off to school ahead of time.

During art time, Michael deliberately sat on the same table as Sally and sat back to back with Freddie. When the children were allowed to talk, Michael started trying to find out about the people who lived on their farm.

"Is your farm very big?" he asked Sally, trying to get the conversation going.

"Yes," said Sally. "It's really big, we've got loads of fields and barns and woods."

"Do you have any animals on the farm?" asked Michael.

"Yes, we've got pigs, cows, sheep and some chickens," she replied.

"It must be hard work looking after a farm," Michael went on, cleverly trying to turn the conversation round towards the people who worked there. "Who does all the work?" he continued.

"Mummy and Daddy," replied Sally.

"That's a lot of work for two people."

"Oh we have other people who help us," Sally replied. "There's Uncle Tony, Trevor, Simon and Will."

"That's quite a few men. Do they live on the farm with you?"

"No, they come on different days, it's just the four of us that live on the farm – well normally it is, but at the moment we have some builders living on the farm with us. They are staying on our farm for a while whilst they change one of our barns into a house for my Nanny and Poppa."

"Wow, it must be busy on your farm at the moment then, how do you all fit into your house?" asked Michael, as he splashed a bit too much paint onto his picture.

"They don't live in the house with us; they are staying in some caravans they brought with them."

Before he had a chance to ask any more questions, the bell rang for break time and the children put down their crayons and paintbrushes and bundled out of the classroom into the playground.

Michael felt very proud of himself indeed and he decided he would make an excellent policeman when he grew up. He couldn't wait to tell the others all that he had found out, so instead of waiting for lunchtime, he hunted them down in the playground during break and told them what he had discovered.

"Great work, Michael," said Luke. "So, we have the four farm workers and the builders as suspects. We need you to find out a few more things, Michael," he continued, thinking quickly.

"Firstly, we need to find out how many builders there are. Next, we need to find out when they are finishing the job because if one of the builders is the burglar and they leave we may never find them. We have to find out how much longer they are staying. Got that Michael?" asked Luke.

"Yep," he said. "This is really fun, I feel like a private instigator."

"You mean private investigator," laughed Whizzo. "You're doing a great job, Michael," he said, encouragingly. "We'll meet back here at lunchtime and see if you have any more information."

So, after many hearty pats on the back, Michael marched off back to his classroom to continue his investigations. To make sure Sally didn't become suspicious, he started to chat to Freddie about life on the farm.

"Freddie, Sally said you've got people building a house for your Nanny and Poppa. That must be a big job. Are there lots of builders?" questioned Michael.

"Nah," said Freddie, whilst vigorously colouring in his drawing of a boat. "There are only four of them."

"Are they staying with you for a long time?" asked Michael.

"They've been with us for ages but they've nearly finished. I think they must be going soon because Nanny and Poppa are coming in two weeks time."

"That will be nice, having your Nanny and Poppa living next to you," said Michael, who, having found out the information he needed, became lost in an exciting conversation about football and who was the best player in the world.

Lunchtime came around and Michael proudly shared the news that there were four builders, who were probably going to be leaving soon, because the job was nearly finished.

"We are going to have to move quickly," said Luke. "I think that after school, two of us need to do a bit of spying to check out the suspects."

"I think that the burglar must be one of the builders," said Whizzo. "It is much more likely that it's one of them, rather than one of the regular farm workers," he continued.

"Luke, I can come with you tonight straight after school," said Tim. "It won't take long for us to cycle there. We can hide our bikes in the hedge at the end of the farm lane and then sneak up round the back through the fields and have a nose around."

"Let's do it," said Luke. "Meet me at my house as soon as you can after school and we'll do a bit of snooping to see what we can find out."

"Can I come too?" asked Michael.

"Sorry but no," said Luke. "If we're snooping around, the fewer of us the better and if we need to make a fast get away, Tim and I can leg it."

So with the plan agreed, the children split up and went their separate ways, with Luke and Tim especially excited about what they might discover in just a few hours time.

Chapter Ten

Big Trouble at Willow Tree Farm

Tim arrived at Luke's house soon after school, wearing his army overalls and ready for adventure.

"Luke, I think we should take some weapons just in case. You never know what we might discover," said Tim.

"Good thinking," said Luke. "I'll go and change into my army gear too and load up two Splodgomatics. I'll also get the Blobomatic with the shoe print on, in case we find any tracks that match."

A few minutes later Luke was back with some ketchup rope tied round his middle, a tube of ketchup glue in his pocket and a Splodgomatic strapped to his back. He handed Tim a Splodgomatic.

"We look like proper soldiers," chuckled Tim. "I'm feeling a bit nervous though. I've never tried to track down a burglar."

"We'll be careful," said Luke. "We won't do anything silly or dangerous, this is just a reconnaissance mission."

"What's that?" asked Tim.

"It means we are just looking around for information. We're not going into battle just yet, the weapons are just a precaution!"

"Right," said Tim. "Come on then, let's go."

"Hold on, take one of these too, it's a walkie talkie, so we can communicate if we have to split up."

"Cool," said Tim. "Go down to the other side of the house and let's see if these bad boys work."

Luke disappeared and Tim switched on his walkie talkie and said, "Come in KK1. Come in KK1, do you read me? This is KK2 ready for action. Do you read me?"

"KK2, this is KK1, I read you loud and clear and I'm ready for action. Meet you in five round the front. Over and out." With that Luke trotted back to the front to see Tim giving him the thumbs up.

"This is soooo cool," said Tim. "Luke and Tim aged ten, on a massive adventure like this with walkie talkies, ketchup weapons and a burglar to chase. We make James Bond look boring," he said, laughing, as the two boys peddled off down the road towards Willow Tree Farm.

It didn't take long for the boys to arrive at the end of the farm lane, where they jumped off their bicycles and dragged them deep into the hedge and out of sight of any passers by. They climbed the gate that lead into the field and started the quarter mile trip towards the farmhouse. They jogged slowly through the field, hugging closely to the hedge so they weren't spotted. After a few minutes, the boys, now breathing hard, slowed down as they arrived at the front garden of the farmhouse. Crouching down, they peered through the hedge to see if they could spot anything. They couldn't see anyone, but they heard the sound of a tractor engine some way off in the distance, and also heard some banging noises which seemed to come from the other side of the farmhouse.

"Let's go round the back of the farmhouse and see what's on the other side," whispered Luke.

"OK," said Tim and with that, they crept alongside the wall that surrounded the farmhouse garden, being careful not to be seen. At the bottom of the garden the wall turned left and they followed it across the back of the garden, until it came to an end and the hedges going across the fields started again. Luke could see a large open area in which there were a number of outbuildings, including a large barn. He saw two men carrying building equipment into the barn, whilst a third man was laying bricks on the ground, obviously building some kind of driveway in front of the barn.

"There are three of our suspects," whispered Luke. "They don't look like burglars. Then again I've never seen a burglar, so I don't really know what one would look like."

"Let's see if we can find the caravans anywhere," said Tim in a low whisper.

The two boys silently carried on walking along the hedge until they got to the end of the farmyard area. In the field beyond, just behind the barns, they spotted two caravans beside a gate. They quickly ran beside the hedge until they were close to the caravan and then threw themselves to the ground to make sure no one could see them.

"Do you think the fourth man is in the caravan?" whispered Tim.

"Not sure. We need to be really...."

Before Luke finished his sentence, one of the caravan doors opened and a man carrying two cups of tea stepped out and started to make his way across the farmyard towards the barn.

"Quick," said Luke. "Now's our chance, let's run and hide under the caravan whilst no one's there. He's left the door open so he must be coming back in a minute."

The boys shot off at top speed and within seconds had dived under the caravan and were lying flat and perfectly still. The only sound they could hear was the noise of their pounding hearts.

From under the caravan they could just see through the gate that led to the farmyard and the barn which was about a minute's walk away from the caravan.

"What do we do now?" asked Tim.

"We stay here until he comes back. He'll probably be back to get more tea or to close the door."

Luke's prediction was spot on because, within a few seconds of disappearing, the man began to come back across the farmyard towards the caravan.

It was at this moment that the two boys realised, probably for the first time, that they were in a very serious situation. If their hunch was right, a dangerous burglar was marching across the farmyard towards them and if they were spotted, they would have a very difficult job explaining what they were doing there. If he searched them and found the Blobomatic with his footprint on, they could really be in trouble. Luke's heart was pounding so hard he thought it was about to burst right out of his chest.

They lay as flat as they could behind the caravan

wheels, hoping and praying that they would not be seen. As he came towards them, his footsteps seemed to boom until he got to the caravan and climbed inside. The relief at not being seen was overwhelming and the boys breathed for the first time in what seemed like minutes.

They heard him moving about in the caravan above them and then, to their amazement, they heard him speaking to someone. After a petrifying moment, thinking that there were two men in the caravan, they realised he was on his mobile phone. Tim pretended to use a mobile phone to explain to Luke what he thought was happening and Luke nodded.

Now, if you are in the middle of an adventure, and you have a crime to solve, sometimes you need a little bit of luck and what happened next was a moment just like that. With the caravan door open, they could hear everything the man said and this is what they heard.

"Trevor, it's Jimmy – how you doing?"

The other man spoke.

"You know we turned over Heston's twice – picked up a nice load of kit, probably worth about sixty grand and some – like taking candy from a baby in this town, no police and no one around at night time. There's one other jeweller in town. We're off on Saturday so we'll have a go on Friday night. We're leaving here at ten o'clock Saturday morning so we'll be back with you around three o'clock in the afternoon with the stuff. We want cash only and we'll have had it valued by the time we get there, so no monkey business."

The other man spoke again.

"Alright, alright, don't get shirty – you know where I'm coming from. Frank and I will see you Saturday."

The conversation ended and the man stepped out of the caravan, shut the door and started walking away back to the barns, leaving the boys breathless, caught between fear and mad excitement.

When the man had disappeared back into the barn Tim said, "Come on, let's get out of here. Quick, whilst he's gone and out of sight."

The boys started to crawl out from under the caravan.

"Wait," said Luke. "Stay here a second, I want to check something."

"What are you going to do?" asked Tim, nervously. "Don't do anything stupid."

Luke quickly crawled out, stood up and then to Tim's utter amazement, he dived into the caravan and closed the door behind him. Tim now heard Luke's footsteps in the caravan above, moving around quickly from one end to the other, he heard things being opened and slammed shut as Luke moved about like lightening, quickly turning things over.

Tim was transfixed by what was going on and it was only when he heard another noise some way off that he cautiously peered out from behind the caravan wheel. To his dismay, the noise he had heard was that of footsteps coming back across the courtyard towards the caravan. The man was returning.

Tim beat his fist on the underside of the caravan and shouted as loud as he dare, "Luke they're coming. Get out fast."

In a second, Luke bolted out of the door and started running across the field back the way they had come. Tim stayed flat on the ground under the caravan, not knowing whether to run and follow Luke, who was some way off already, or to stay still.

He heard the man shout and saw him start to give chase. His face was red with anger as he sped full pelt across the farmyard, whilst Luke hurtled across the field, running faster than he had ever done before in his life. Luke disappeared round a corner and out of sight, just before the man came out of the farmyard into the field. The man stopped. He was panting and breathing heavily, whilst looking across the field to see if he could see any trace of the boy who had been in the caravan. He stepped into the caravan to check if anything had gone missing. Suddenly, Tim heard a roar from inside the caravan and the man jumped out and set off down the field, giving chase once again. Thankfully, Luke was long gone and he had managed to find a hiding place deep inside a dense hedge, where he lay perfectly still, with no plans to move from there for a very long time.

Chapter Eleven
Battle Plans

"Come in KK1, do you read me KK1? I repeat, do you read me? This is Tim, over."

"KK2, this is KK1, I read you. Are you okay?"

"I'm still under the caravan. The man has disappeared across the field to look for you. Where are you?"

"I'm in a hedge about half way back to the bikes. I can't see him anywhere."

"Luke, you're bonkers. I thought you said this was a reconnaissance trip only. Now we're in real trouble. Wait…. the man is on his way back to the caravan. Over and out."

The man was trudging back towards the caravan, looking hot, sweaty and furious. He shouted for Frank across the farmyard and a man came out of the barn and started walking towards the caravan.

Tim's heart started pounding again as the two men approached the caravan from different directions. They eventually met and stood by the caravan door, leaving Tim with a clear view of their ankles and feet.

"What's happened, Jimmy?" asked the man.

"I found some kid in the caravan. He's only gone and stolen the jewels we nabbed from Heston's. Something funny is goin' on 'ere and I don't like it Frank, I don't like it one bit. How did the kid know we got jewels in 'ere? I've been off looking for him but he's gone. He could be anywhere by now."

The other man said some very rude words and then said, "Did he get all of them?"

"No, one bag only, the other one is still under the bed," said Jimmy.

"Good. Look, he was probably just a kid looking to nick some money and got lucky and found our jewels," said Frank. "No one knows about us, the police ain't shown up so if the police ain't on to us, you ain't telling me no kid has tracked us down?"

"I hope you're right Frank, but it is a bit odd. We've got stolen kit in the caravan and a kid comes from nowhere and steals it! Tell me that's not odd!"

"Look, we're out of here on Saturday. We'll just have to make sure we get an extra good haul of jewels on Friday night. It'll be alright. Trust me."

"Let's get in the van and have a drive round, see if

we can find that kid. He must have to go somewhere using a road. Come on. Oh yeah, and lock the caravan, in case he comes back to try his luck again."

The men locked the caravan door and started walking back to the barn. When Tim felt they were a safe distance, he was back on the walkie talkie.

"KK1, this is KK2, do you read me?"

"KK2 I'm listening, are you okay?" said Luke.

"Yes, the coast is clear but the men are going to get in their van and come and look for us. I'll meet you back at the bikes a.s.a.p., but don't go by the road. Stay near the bikes in the bushes until I get to you. Over and out," said Tim.

Tim carefully crept out from under the caravan and shot off back towards the bikes, keeping close to the hedge the whole way. He eventually met up with Luke near the bikes who was crouching in the bushes and out of sight, in case the men came down the farm lane and spotted him.

"You're bonkers," said Tim. "We nearly got caught. That was mad going into the caravan."

"I know, I'm sorry," said Luke, "but I just had to check if the jewels were in there and look what I found!"

Luke pulled a small cloth bag out from under his jacket and opened it up to reveal a sparkling array of the finest jewellery either of them had seen; necklaces, earrings, watches, rings, and gold pens in abundance.

For a moment Tim was spellbound by the sparkling jewels.

"Wow Luke, we may not have caught the burglars but we have got back some of the stolen items. Jake's dad is going to be well chuffed with us. I heard the men say that there's another bigger bag of jewels under the bed. You may be bonkers Luke but what a result!"

"I saw the men go by in the van. It's a white one with the words **Framptons Builders** written down the side in blue."

"We'll have to push our bikes back through the fields and woods," said Tim. "It's way too risky to go back by the road."

So the boys, carefully guarding the jewels, set off back home through the fields that led to the woods near to Luke's house. There was only one road to cross and when they got to it, the boys made doubly sure there was no van coming, before crossing at top speed and dashing into the safety of Luke's road.

Relieved and hungry, the boys arrived home, exhausted from all the excitement and desperate to tell the others all that had happened.

Later that night, Michael sat on Luke's bed with his hands full of jewels.

"Tell me everything that happened again, Luke," asked Michael, who had already heard the story twice but wanted to hear it for a third time.

Luke went through the story one more time, with Michael asking questions throughout. He especially liked the bit when the two boys were under the caravan, overhearing the plans for the next robbery.

"Were you scared, Luke? I think I would have been," said Michael.

"I was a little bit," confessed Luke. "It was exciting and scary at the same time. I was just really glad they didn't get Tim after I had gone, that would have been awful."

"Lights out, boys," came a command from downstairs. "No more talking please, it's late."

Michael scampered back to his bedroom and Luke clambered into bed with the jewels safely tucked under his duvet. What a day it had been. They were without doubt in the middle of an amazing adventure and he knew there was more to come.

The next day at school during break time, Luke and Tim told Whizzo and Sarah all about their adventures of the previous evening. Whizzo and Sarah listened, with eyes wide open. They almost wouldn't have believed the story had Luke not produced one sparkling diamond from his pocket and passed it round for each of them to hold.

"It's not fair," moaned Whizzo. "I've missed out on the best part of the adventure."

"I'm glad I wasn't under the caravan," said Sarah. "That would have been so scary."

"It was scary, actually," said Tim, "but not half as scary as it was when Luke disappeared into the caravan and I saw the man walking back towards us."

"So, where are they going to burgle next?" asked Michael.

"Well," said Luke, "they said there was one other jewellery shop in town so it must be Crowns at the end of the High Street."

"When shall we tell the police?" asked Sarah.

"When we've caught the burglars of course!" said Tim. "We've got some of the jewels back, we know who the burglars are, we just need to catch them now and then our job will be done," he continued in a very important tone of voice.

"And how are we going to do that?" asked Sarah. "We can't stay up all night on Friday and we are hardly likely to be able to stop two grown men anyway."

"I've got an idea," said Whizzo. "Why don't we spy on the shop and take photos of them doing the burglary?"

"That would mean us staying up very late though and we can't do that. It would be too dangerous," replied Sarah.

"I've got it," said Luke triumphantly. "What we'll do is go back to the caravan and leave them a note saying if they want their jewels back, they need to meet us in the woods at six o'clock Friday evening, at the place they hid their burglar's kit. Then we will lie in wait for them, ambush them and attack them using our ketchup weapons!"

"Perfect!" said Tim gleefully.

"What if we get in to big trouble?" asked Sarah.

"One of us can leg it back up to the house and call the police!" said Luke.

"Sounds great to me," said Tim, already desperate to unleash his ketchup spray gun on the burglars. "We'll need to set up some traps, and load up with all our ketchup weapons. Boy, are they going to get it from me!"

For the rest of the lunch break the children plotted

and schemed. They drew diagrams of the woods and agreed who was going to be stationed where and talked about how they were finally going to catch the burglars and hand them over to the police.

Later that evening after school, Whizzo, having missed out on the first adventure, was given the job of leaving a note on the caravan door telling the men about the Friday six o'clock rendezvous to get their jewels back.

Whizzo had written the note which simply said:-

If you want your jewels back, meet me in the woods where you hid your burglar's kit at six o'clock on Friday.
From the boy who found them in your caravan.

Whizzo went through the fields, following the directions Luke had given him. He waited to check no one was around and when he was absolutely sure the coast was clear, he stuck the note on the caravan door and then disappeared at top speed, without being spotted.

When the two men found the note, they had a big argument. Frank wanted to meet the boy and get the jewels back, but Jimmy was worried.

"This ain't for real Frank. A kid comes and nicks the jewels we nicked, and then offers to give them back. It's a set up." said Jimmy.

"Set up or no set up," said Frank, "no kid is going to get the better of me. Anyway, I reckon Trevor is involved somewhere in this, he's the only one who knows we had the stuff here. He must be involved somehow."

"I reckon the kid found our kit and somehow tracked us back here," said Jimmy.

"Well it must be some amazingly smart kid who tracks us down when the police can't do it. I'm going to meet this kid and find out who's working with him," said Frank obstinately. "And you're going to have to come with me in case the kid is with someone."

Eventually, the two burglars decided they would go to the woods at six o'clock on Friday to get their jewels back. Unbeknown to them, the Ketchup Kids would be waiting patiently, fully armed and ready for battle.

Chapter Twelve
War in the Woods

When Friday finally came, the children felt both frantic with excitement and scared at the same time. Sarah was especially nervous, but she didn't want to show it because she wanted to play just as much a part in the adventure as the boys. She couldn't help thinking about how awful it would be if one of them got injured in the battle, or even worse, was kidnapped.

It was half past five and the children were all in the tree house, kitted out in their army overalls and armed with their ketchup weapons.

Luke pulled out the map he had drawn with everyone's positions marked on it with a cross. He pointed at the map with a stick.

"Right, is everyone feeling okay before I go through this one more time," he said.

Everyone nodded seriously.

"My tummy feels funny," said Michael. "It feels like it's twisting and turning inside me."

"You've got butterflies," said Tim. "It's the feeling you get when you are excited and nervous about something, like when you are about to blast burglars with ketchup!"

"OK," said Luke. "Sarah, your position is here at the top of the path, armed with your bow and arrow and hidden in the laurel bush. When you see the men coming, call me on the walkie talkie."

"OK," said Sarah.

"Tim, your position is inside the hollow tree to the south of the hole, you're to stay in there until I give you the call to attack. Got that?"

"Yep," said Tim, as he confidently stroked his spray gun with a glint in his eye.

"Michael, do you know where you are?"

"Here," he said, pointing to the map. "Up the tree above the hole and loaded up with two jumbo ketchup bombs and a hand grenade ketchup bomb."

"Good," said Luke. "When you think you have got a perfect shot, you drop the bombs. It's up to you when you do it."

"OK," said Michael, already enjoying the thought of scoring a direct hit on the burglars' heads.

"Whizzo, you are positioned here, inside the holly bush about five metres from the hole, with your Splodgomatic. They will never expect an attack from inside there. I'm here, up in the tree so I can swing down and try and take one of them out. I'll have some ketchup rope and a Splodgomatic. Sarah, once you hear us attacking, run down to help and as soon as we've got them under control, or if we look like we're in trouble, run back up to the house and telephone the police. Clear?"

"Yes," said Sarah.

"Right guys, this is it. Check your weapons and let's get into position!"

The children climbed down from the tree house and went through the gate and into the woods. Sarah disappeared off up the path to bury herself deep inside the laurel bush, whilst Tim and Whizzo helped Michael climb the tree above the hole. Tim passed up his two jumbo ketchup bombs, which were so big and heavy they had to lift them up in plastic bags one at a time.

When Michael was safely in position, Tim, Whizzo and Luke scurried off to their posts. Luke swiftly climbed up into his appointed tree and from his lofty viewpoint he could see the whole battlefield. Whizzo gave a few gasps of pain as he wriggled his way into the holly bush, whilst Tim slid silently into the hollow tree and out of sight.

It was quarter to six and all they had to do now was to wait.

In the silence of the woods, with all the children hidden from view, everyone now felt a little bit scared. As the minutes ticked away, they were all suffering from butterflies as they waited for the enemy to arrive.

Sarah was breathing so heavily she thought that when the men came by, they would be bound to hear her. As she waited, she kept reminding herself to keep calm. She looked at her watch again. It said three minutes to six. "They'll be coming soon," she thought, and just at that moment she heard men's voices in the distance. The voices gradually became louder and louder and she could hear their footsteps coming closer. She sat motionless, and held her breath as the two men walked past, no more than a few feet away. As soon as they had gone by, she breathed a gigantic sigh of relief and she got straight on to the walkie talkie.

"Luke it's me, the men have just gone past. They'll be with you in under a minute," she whispered.

"Message received Sarah. Over and out."

"They're on their way," whispered Luke from the tree, loud enough to be heard by the children, but not so loud that the men would hear.

Luke saw the men coming down the path and into the small clearing where the hole was.

"No sign of the boy, Frank and it's six o'clock. He's probably taking the mickey out of us. I bet he doesn't show up."

"Let's have a look in the hole and see if our stuff's in there," said Frank.

He bent down and felt inside the hole. It was at that point that Michael spotted his opportunity. As he peered down on his target, he was in the perfect position to launch the first attack.

"Three," he whispered to himself and started raising his arms.

"Two," he said as he took careful aim.

"One," he said preparing himself for the throw of his life.

"Now!" he yelled.

Michael hurled the jumbo ketchup bomb, which fell with a huge force and smashed on to the man's back, dramatically exploding on impact and sending him sprawling to the ground.

Jimmy shrieked in surprise and pain, not having the faintest clue what had happened. Frank looked up in the tree from where the bomb had been launched but couldn't see Michael hiding in the branches. As he stared at Jimmy covered in something red and messy he angrily cried, "What the blazes was that?"

Before Jimmy or Frank could say anything more, Michael launched his second jumbo bomb aiming another perfect shot, but this time striking Frank directly on his head! The ketchup bomb exploded again, causing Frank to totter around in a complete daze, with his head and shoulders soaked in ketchup.

The next thing they heard was a voice from the skies shouting, "Attack, attack, attack!"

Jimmy leaped up, realising they were in some sort of danger. As soon as he was on his feet, he heard a scream and suddenly he felt two feet planted squarely on his back. He was hit with such a force he was pushed forward hard and ended up head butting the tree in front of him and falling to the ground.

Frank whirled round in anger looking to see who had attacked them and saw Luke standing there with his Splodgomatic aiming right at him. Luke pulled the trigger and a torrent of ketchup splattered the man full on the face. He roared again in anger and lunged towards Luke making a grab for him. Luke dodged the man, who then stumbled onto the ground. Before he had a chance to stand up, he felt a foot come down on his chest. As he looked up, he found himself staring at a boy, dressed in army overalls and pointing some kind of gadget at his face. It was Tim who had appeared from the hollow tree. He was ready for battle!

"Eat this, bad guy," said Tim, who fired his spray gun straight into the man's face, filling the man's mouth and nostrils with ketchup.

With Frank being pummelled by Tim, Whizzo

lunged out from the holly bush, screaming like a madman and started shooting at Jimmy, who was just beginning to recover from his collision with the tree.

Meanwhile, Frank, now enraged, managed to yank Tim's foot and throw him off. He stood up yelling and managed to grab Whizzo around his neck to stop him attacking Jimmy.

"Let go, you thief, let go," Whizzo cried, as he struggled to break free.

"No way, you little brat, not until you give us our jewels back," said Frank.

At that moment, with Whizzo firmly locked in the grip of Frank, an arrow flew through the air and planted itself on Frank's forehead. He yelled in pain and Whizzo, seeing his opportunity to escape, stamped hard on the man's foot.

"Great shot, Sarah!" shouted Whizzo, gratefully as he broke free from the man's grip.

Not knowing the arrow had been laced with Whizzo's ketchup super glue, Frank could not pull the arrow off his forehead and Sarah, celebrating the success of her first shot, fired a second arrow, this time striking Frank directly on the chin. Frank now had two arrows welded to his face, one on his forehead and the other on his chin.

"I'm going to kill you kids," he shouted, now mad with rage. "Jimmy, take one of the kids hostage!"

Jimmy was still in recovery mode. He had been hit by a jumbo ketchup bomb, had smacked his head into a tree and been covered in ketchup from Whizzo's Splodgomatic and at that moment was trying to get ketchup out of his eyes. Luke threw one end of his ketchup rope to Whizzo.

"Quick Whizzo, help me tie up Jimmy. Sarah, run for the police!"

Sarah shot off of like a rocket whilst the two boys ran round Jimmy, travelling in opposite directions. The boys circled him four times, pinning his arms to his body and tying his legs together, so he couldn't run. With his arms and legs out of action, he was easily pushed to the ground. The children sat on him and started to tie knots around his hands and feet and then began to secure him to a tree trunk so he could not escape.

Suddenly, Luke heard Tim shouting. He looked up to see Tim under attack from Frank, who had found a large stick and was moving towards Tim with a menacing look in his eye.

"I need help guys, quick, I can't hold him off much longer!" shouted Tim who was still firing ketchup at the fast approaching Frank.

"Whizzo, finish tying up Jimmy, I'll help Tim."

Luke, seeing his friend in real danger, ran towards Tim at top speed, shouting like a Viking warrior.

"Leave him alone!" shouted Luke, as he unleashed further powerful jets of ketchup at Frank. Frank spun round to face Luke and started trying to clobber him with his stick. All of a sudden they heard a voice above them.

"Hey mister," came a cry from a tree.

Frank looked up and as he did, Michael launched a ketchup grenade and with a mighty force hit Frank on the bridge of his nose. Ketchup spurted into his eyes and he began to spin around aimlessly, yelling in pain.

"Quick Tim, now's our chance, take the rope!" shouted Luke.

Tim grabbed the rope, and using the same trick as before, the two boys ran round the man in opposite directions, circling him until he was unable to move his arms. Before they could tie his legs though, Frank started to run, realising that he was on the verge of being caught. Just as it looked as if he was about to escape, Whizzo appeared from nowhere and with one glorious rugby tackle from behind, brought the man down. Within seconds, the three boys piled on top of him to stop him from standing up again.

Michael jumped down from the tree to join in the fun and shouted "Bundle!" as he launched himself through the air and onto the pile of bodies. Luke set to work, securely tying up Frank's feet to prevent a further attempt to run away.

At last both men were safely captured. As they lay on the floor cursing the children, the boys jumped around with elation, hugging each other and cheering loudly.

"We caught the bad guys," yelled Michael at the top of his voice.

He marched over to one of the men, pointed at him and said;

"Hey mister, you're in big trouble now. That will teach you to steal jewels and stuff from our friend."

The two men continued to shout abuse at them, frustrated, angry and still not quite sure how they had ended up being caught and trapped by a bunch of children. Bound in rope, covered in ketchup and in a complete mess, they simply couldn't believe what had happened to them. It seemed they were caught up in some strange nightmare.

As the boys were laughing and savouring their victory, they suddenly heard a stampede of footsteps coming towards them. Sarah arrived with Mr and Mrs Kingsman and two burly police officers.

"Goodness me," said one of the officers. "What have we here? Looks like we've got ourselves a right mess! Would someone like to tell me what's been going on?"

The children stood there, holding their weapons, looking happy but exhausted.

"These are really bad people who steal things and so we caught them for you, so they could go to prison!" said Michael.

"Let's go back to the house and then perhaps you can explain exactly what has been going on," said Mr Kingsman, looking very concerned.

"Sounds good to me," said Tim, still buzzing with excitement from the battle. "I need a drink and some food after all that action."

The others heartily agreed with Tim and so they marched back up to the house, with Jimmy and Frank now in the safekeeping of the police. The two crooks were handcuffed and locked in the back of the police van.

When they had settled inside the house, Luke was tasked with telling the police about all that had happened. He told them about how they had found the burglars' bag and tracked them down using a Blobomatic and about how they had been to the caravan and found the jewels. At this point, Luke's mum went ashen white and nearly fainted. He told them about how they had laid the trap for Jimmy and Frank and eventually caught them and tied them up. The police could hardly believe what they were hearing! When Luke produced the Blobomatic with the burglar's shoeprint on it, and the crowbar containing traces of blue paint, the police were speechless and full of admiration. And when the children finally revealed the bag of jewels, the police cheered and gave the Ketchup Kids a raucous round of applause!

Luke's mum was so proud of them that she ran over and gave each of them an enormous hug. She simply couldn't believe what had happened. But then again, neither could the Ketchup Kids!

Epilogue
Fame and Fortune!

The children sat on the couch, facing the television in eager anticipation. It was just before ten o'clock in the evening and all their parents were there, as were Mr and Mrs Heston and Jake, who had been invited along for a celebratory drink.

"Shh, Shh," said Luke. "It's about to start."

First there was music and then the newsreader appeared.

"Good evening, this is the Ten O'Clock News from the BBC. Earlier this evening in the small town of Hambleside, Buckinghamshire, an extraordinary story unfolded when a group of children who call themselves the Ketchup Kids managed to track down and catch some jewellery thieves, using nothing more than some rather unusual ketchup weapons."

The newsreader went on.

"Jimmy Frampton and Frank Carruthers had twice burgled a local jewellery shop, and in spite of the police finding no clues as to who had carried out the crime, the Ketchup Kids tracked the thieves down and lured them into a trap where they managed to apprehend them. The local police were stunned to be presented with the two criminals, who were handed over to them at 6.15 pm this evening."

The news item continued for about two or three more minutes and the BBC showed pictures of Jimmy and Frank covered in ketchup and tied up in ketchup rope. There were also interviews with each of the children, during which the children laughed uncontrollably because Tim kept pulling funny faces at the camera whenever he appeared on screen!

When the news finished, Tim laughed and said, "Ah what it is to be famous! I probably won't be able to go to school on Monday because I'll be swamped by fans!"

"In your dreams," said Sarah. "The only thing you'll be famous for is for looking weird on telly!"

"No, that's not true," said Luke interjecting. "He'll be famous for looking weird on telly *and* for being part of the awesome and amazing, crime stopping, burglar catching, Ketchup Kids!"

Luke asked everyone in turn what their best bit of the adventure had been. Luke's favourite part was finding the diamonds in the caravan, whilst Sarah's was scoring two direct hits on Frank's head to help free Whizzo from being strangled. Whizzo said his favourite part was discovering the ketchup blobs outside the jewellery shop. Tim had two favourite moments, being on television and getting a £200 reward which he was going to spend on a new bike, some sweets and more supplies of ketchup for their next adventure. Michael said it was totally impossible to have a favourite part because it was all brilliant, but if he had to choose one, it would be when he launched the jumbo bombs on the bad guys.

"Do you think we'll ever have another adventure?" asked Michael, hopefully.

"Probably not," said Luke. "We're very lucky to have had one great adventure. Most children don't have any adventures at all."

"I think we'll have loads more," said Tim. "I bet we even get a telephone call tomorrow from the Prime Minister, asking us to help him catch some even badder people than the ones we caught. Besides, I could do with another £200 reward!"

"Dream on, Tim, dream on," chuckled Luke. "Who knows though, you may be right, maybe one day we will have another adventure and if we did, we would surely be the luckiest children in the whole world!"

If you want to have some more fun with
The Ketchup Kids
go to
www.theketchupkids.com